To Mulford Page Radlauer

A Winter Day
by Douglas Florian

SCHOLASTIC INC.
New York Toronto London Auckland Sydney

ISBN 0-590-44386-0

Copyright © 1987 by Douglas Florian.
All rights reserved. Published by Scholastic Inc.,
730 Broadway, New York, NY 10003, by arrangement with
William Morrow & Company, Inc.

12 11 10 9 8 7 6 5   1 2 3 4 5 6/9

Printed in the U.S.A.   34

First Scholastic printing, January 1991

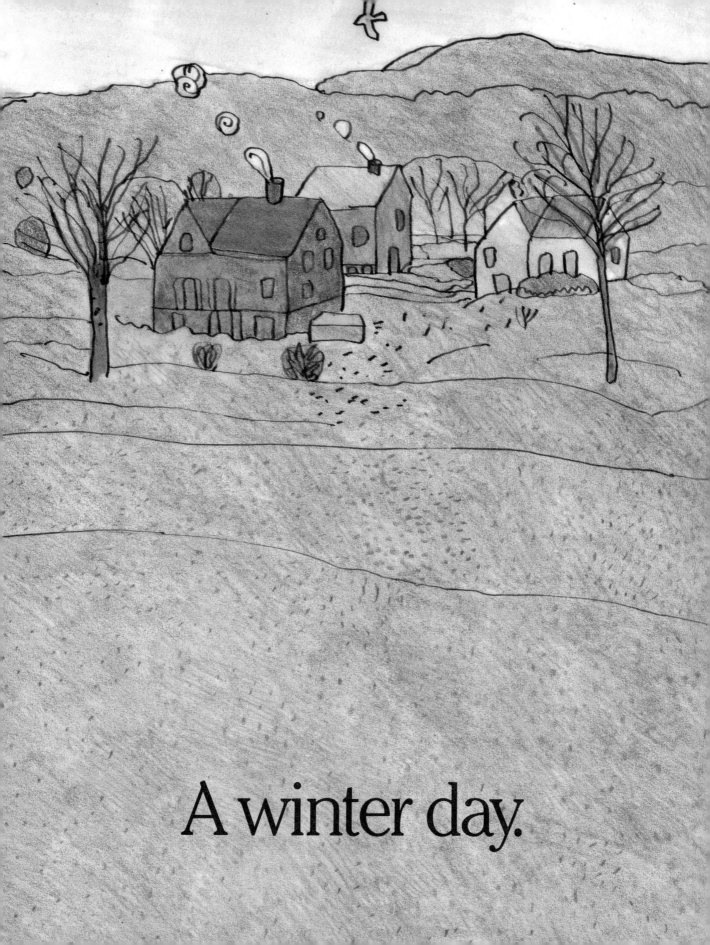

A winter day.

Cold and gray.

Snowflakes.

Pancakes.

Cover your heads.

Skates and sleds.

A snowball grows.

Warm your toes.

Everything white.

Orange light.

A winter night.